Staying at Sam's
Text copyright © 1989 by Jenny Hessell
Illustrations copyright © 1989 by Jenny Williams
First published by
William Collins Sons & Co. Ltd., London.
Printed in Belgium. All rights reserved.
10 9 8 7 6 5 4 3 2 1
First American Edition, 1990

Library of Congress Cataloging-in-Publication Data
Hessell, Jenny.
    Staying at Sam's / Jenny Hessell ; illustrated by
Jenny Williams.
        p.   cm.
Summary: When he spends the night at his friend
Sam's, a young boy discovers that his family's way of
doing things is not necessarily the way all families do
things.
    ISBN 0-397-32432-4 : $
    ISBN 0-397-32433-2 (lib. bdg.) : $
    [1. Family life—Fiction.] I. Williams, Jenny,
1939– ill. II. Title.
PZ7.H4365St 1990   89-14561
[E]—dc20   CIP
                                                AC

STAYING AT SAM'S

Jenny Hessell

illustrated by

Jenny Williams

J. B. LIPPINCOTT
NEW YORK

Staying at Sam's house is like
visiting another planet.

You wouldn't *believe* the things they do.

First, there's all the kissing.
It starts as soon as you walk in the door.

Sam kisses his mom.

Then he kisses the baby.

Then Grandma comes in and kisses Sam.

Then Sam kisses the cat.

When Sam's dad comes home,
it starts all over again.

Sam's dad kisses Sam's mom.

And Sam.

And Grandma.

Then they all kiss the baby.

I've never seen so much kissing in
one family, not even on holidays.
In my family, hardly anyone kisses.

Sometimes Dad hugs me if he
hasn't seen me for a while.

And Mom gives me a cuddle
when she tucks me in.

But the last time I was kissed
was on my birthday –
and that was years ago!

At Sam's you're lucky if they keep it down to

a kiss a minute.

Then there's the bathroom.

At my place, if you want to have a bath,
you go to the bathroom by yourself.
Then you shut the door.

And *then* you take your clothes off.

At Sam's place, it all happens
the other way around.

Nobody waits till
they're in the
bathroom before
they start
getting undressed.

And nobody shuts the door.
They just don't bother.

Once, Sam even sat on the edge of the bath,
talking to his mom while she washed.
You wouldn't see that happening at
our place in a million years!

But the craziest thing of all is their family bed.
At home, I'm not allowed in the big bed.

My mom says, "Big beds are for big people. Little beds are for little people."

I don't think Sam's parents know about this rule, because they let *anyone* into their bed.

Sam, the baby, the cat – even me.

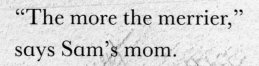

"The more the merrier,"
says Sam's mom.

Last time I went to Sam's, I said,
"How about coming to stay
at our place next weekend?"
"Great," said Sam.
"It's always fun at your house.
Kind of like being on
another planet."